WREATH
OF
ERIN

D1011152

Of all Charles Dickens' famous works, the story of
Oliver Twist must rank very high in its appeal to both
children and grown ups. Who can resist following
Oliver through the twists and turns of his fortunes, as
he meets the evil Fagin and Bill Sikes; the Artful
Dodger and brave Nancy? Victorian London comes to
life in this gripping tale.

First edition

© LADYBIRD BOOKS LTD MCMLXXXIV

*All rights reserved. No part of this publication may be reproduced, stored in a retrieval
system, or transmitted in any form or by any means, electronic, mechanical, photo-
copying, recording or otherwise, without the prior consent of the copyright owner.*

OLIVER TWIST

by Charles Dickens

retold by Brenda Ralph Lewis

with illustrations by Gwen Tourret

Ladybird Books Loughborough

Oliver Twist

Oliver Twist sat wearily on the doorstep.
He shivered. The sun was just rising over
the town and the chill of the night was still
in the empty streets. Oliver was too
exhausted to move. He had walked seventy
long hard miles since running away from
Mr Sowerberry, his employer, and his feet
were sore and bleeding. He ached all over,
and he was thin and pale from hunger.

Still, Oliver thought, he was glad he had
run away. Mr Sowerberry had threatened to
send him back to where he came from: the
workhouse. The workhouse was a frightful
place where the inmates were punished
severely for the slightest thing, and there
was never enough food to eat. A hundred
years ago and more, the poorest of poor
people lived in the workhouse. Oliver, who
was nine years old, had never known any
other home, for he was born and brought up
there. He did not even know who his mother
was, for she had died soon after his birth.

An hour or two passed, and people began
appearing in the streets of the town. They
glanced at the exhausted little orphan sitting
on the doorstep, but most of them glanced
away and hurried on.

Then, all of a sudden, Oliver felt someone
was staring hard at him. A snub-nosed,
rough looking boy was standing close by,
looking him up and down with sharp, ugly
little eyes.

'Hello!' the boy greeted Oliver chirpily.
'What are you doing here?'

'I'm hungry and tired. I've been walking
for seven days!' Oliver replied in a weak
voice.

The boy whistled in wonderment. 'Seven
days!' he exclaimed. Then, unexpectedly,
he gave Oliver a kind look. 'You'll be
wanting grub. Don't worry, I'll pay!'

The boy was as good as his word, and when Oliver had wolfed down the first real meal he had had for days, he asked: 'Going to London?'

'Yes,' Oliver told him.

'Got any lodgings?'

'No,' said Oliver ruefully.

'I suppose you want some place to sleep tonight, then?' said the boy.

Oliver nodded. 'I do indeed!'

'I know a nice old gent in London who'll give you a bed for nothing — he knows me very well!' The boy sounded very confident.

This offer of a place to sleep, and a free place at that, was very tempting and Oliver accepted gratefully.

'What's your name?' the boy wanted to know.

Oliver told him.

'Mine's Jack Dawkins — they call me the Artful Dodger!' the boy said, as if he were proud of it.

Oliver was none too sure that someone with a name like that was an honest person, but he was so grateful for the Dodger's help that he said nothing.

What Oliver Twist did not know yet was that the Dodger belonged to a gang of pickpockets and robbers. Nor did he know that the old gentleman referred to, whose name was Fagin, was the ringleader of the gang.

Fagin's house was in a very old part of London and Oliver and the Artful Dodger had to walk through a maze of dark, smelly streets to reach it. Oliver found that frightening enough, but he was even more scared when he met Fagin. Fagin was a very old, shrivelled-up creature with a villainous-looking face and a mass of matted red hair.

'Come in, come in, my boy!' Fagin welcomed Oliver after the Dodger had introduced him. 'We're very glad to see you, very!'

There was something about Fagin's voice that made Oliver feel cold all over, but the old man seemed kind enough. He gave Oliver a meal, and when he grew drowsy, showed him to an old mattress where he could sleep.

In the days that followed, the Dodger and other young boys in Fagin's gang went out picking pockets. They brought back large numbers of handkerchiefs, pocket books and other objects which Oliver was given to sort out. Oliver, however, did not suspect that these things were stolen until one day, he was allowed to go out with the Dodger and another young pickpocket called Charley Bates.

The boys seemed to wander aimlessly through the streets for a long time until, suddenly, the Dodger halted in a narrow passageway and drew his companions back against the wall.

'See that old fellow by the bookstall?' the Dodger whispered. He pointed to a gentleman on the other side of the passageway who looked very prosperous. He wore gold spectacles and a velvet jacket.

'He'll do!' muttered the Artful Dodger.

'Very nicely!' agreed Charley Bates.

The two boys slipped across the passageway to where the old gentleman stood reading a book he had picked up. As Oliver watched in growing alarm, the Artful Dodger plunged his hand into the old

gentleman's pocket, drew out a
handkerchief and handed it to Charley. Then
the two of them ran full speed round the
corner and out of sight, leaving Oliver
standing open-mouthed.

Oliver felt a tingle of terror at what he had
seen. It was out and out stealing, and he
was involved! Oliver began to run away as
fast as he could, but he was too late. The
old gentleman, whose name was
Mr Brownlow, put his hand in his pocket,
discovered that his handkerchief was
missing and began shouting, 'Stop! Stop,
thief!' He set off after the fleeing Oliver,
and was joined by a growing crowd of
people. A big, rough-looking man soon

overtook Oliver and gave him a hefty blow with his fist. Oliver fell sprawling in the mud.

Someone called a policeman, and Oliver was bundled off to the nearest police station. Mr Brownlow followed. Curiously, he seemed to regret the whole business, and said so when Oliver was taken before the magistrate, Mr Fang.

'This boy is not a thief, sir, I'm sure of it!' Mr Brownlow protested. 'Please deal kindly with him! Besides, I believe he is ill!'

Oliver did, indeed, look very unwell. All of a sudden, he fell to the floor in a faint.

Just then, an elderly man came rushing into the courtroom. 'Stop! Stop!' he cried.

'Who are you?' Mr Fang demanded crossly.

'I keep the bookstall in the passageway!' the newcomer explained. 'The robbery was committed by another boy, not this poor young fellow!' He pointed to Oliver, who still lay unconscious on the floor.

Mr Fang frowned, and started grumbling about people wasting his valuable time. He could do nothing, of course, except dismiss the charge against Oliver. Oliver was thrown onto the pavement outside the courtroom, where Mr Brownlow found him.

'Dear me, how pale he is! And he's shivering! He has a fever, I'll be bound!' Mr Brownlow bent down beside Oliver, regarding him anxiously. 'Call a coach, somebody, directly!'

The next thing Oliver knew was that he was in bed in a quiet, shady room. 'What place is this?' he murmured.

Oliver spoke feebly, but someone heard him. A plump, motherly looking old lady appeared beside the bed. There was a sweet, loving expression on her face.

'Hush, dear!' she said softly. 'You must stay quiet now, or you will be ill again!'

The lady's name was Mrs Bedwin and she was Mr Brownlow's housekeeper. For several more days, she looked after Oliver and saw to his every need, until at last the boy was well enough for Mr Brownlow to visit him.

'And how do you feel now, dear boy?' the old gentleman wanted to know.

'Oh, much better, sir, and very happy — very grateful indeed for all your goodness to me!'

As Oliver spoke, Mr Brownlow kept staring at him. This poor neglected little

waif reminded him of someone, but who? Then, the answer came to him. Of course, the portrait! Mr Brownlow looked up at the picture hanging on the wall just above Oliver's head. It showed a very pretty young lady. Mr Brownlow glanced at Oliver again and gave a start.

'Mrs Bedwin!' he gasped. 'Don't you see? This boy — his eyes, his mouth, his expression, his whole face, is the same as the face in the picture!'

*   *   *

Meanwhile, the Artful Dodger and Charley had been in big trouble with Fagin for 'losing' Oliver in the street.

When they returned without him, Fagin flew into a rage and threatened to throttle both of them. Oliver now knew quite a lot about the gang and Fagin was worried in case the boy had 'peached' — that is, betrayed the gang to the police.

'He must be found, he must!' Fagin stormed.

'But.. but how?' Charley Bates stuttered. 'London's an enormous place, Fagin. Where do we start?'

Fagin's fury suddenly faded away. A cunning gleam came into his eyes. 'Leave that to me, my boy,' he told Charley. 'I'll think of something!'

Fagin did not take long to come up with a plan. One of the thieves in the gang was a girl called Nancy, and Fagin told her to go to the police station to see what she could find out about Oliver.

At first Nancy refused, for she was afraid of the police. She was more afraid, though, of Bill Sikes, a brutal bully of a man who was another member of Fagin's gang.

'Say No, would you?' Bill glowered at Nancy, and raised his hand. 'You'll get my fist in your face!' he threatened.

It would not have been the first time Bill had beaten Nancy up. 'All right, all right,' she said hastily. 'I'll go!'

If she had to run this errand, Nancy thought, she might as well make a good job of it. Nancy was a good actress and when she got to the police station, she burst into tears. Through her wails and sobs, she told the police officer that she had lost her dear little brother. She meant Oliver, of course.

'Where is he, oh, where is he?' Nancy wept. 'I must find him, I must!'

The police officer was a soft-hearted man, and he was totally deceived by Nancy's pretence. So he told her that the boy had been taken away by an old gentleman who lived somewhere near Pentonville in north London.

When Nancy returned with this news, Fagin at once sent her out again, together with the Artful Dodger and Charley Bates, to search for the house in Pentonville.

'Oliver has not betrayed us yet!' Fagin muttered nervously. 'Nancy would've learned at the station had he done that! But he must be found before he can talk, or we are all lost!'

Oliver was going to fall into Fagin's hands much more easily than anyone thought. As he slowly recovered his health, he tried to think of some way to repay all the loving care he had received in Mr Brownlow's house. Oliver's chance came one day when a messenger delivered a parcel of books for Mr Brownlow, but left before he could be given some other old volumes which Mr Brownlow had wanted to return to the shop.

'Please let me take them, sir!' Oliver begged. 'I won't be ten minutes! I'll run all the way!'

Oliver's eyes sparkled with eagerness and Mr Brownlow could not refuse him. So he gave Oliver the books and a five pound note to pay a bill for him at the bookshop.

Oliver set off briskly. He felt very smart in the new set of clothes Mr Brownlow had bought for him.

They were the first new clothes Oliver had ever worn, for in the workhouse, there were only the old clothes people had discarded. Oliver never knew how many other workhouse boys had worn them before him, but it must have been a great many, because they were always ragged and torn.

Oliver had nearly reached the bookshop when all of a sudden a young woman stepped into his path. She flung her arms round his neck and to his amazement started crying: 'Oh, my gracious! I've found him! My dear lost little brother! I've found him!'

It was Nancy. She had just come out of a public house where she had left Fagin and Bill Sikes drinking and talking together. She was holding on to Oliver very tightly, and he struggled hard, trying to escape.

'You're not my sister! You're not! I haven't got a sister!' Oliver kept yelling.

Just then, he felt Mr Brownlow's books being snatched from him, and a heavy blow landed on the back of his head. Bill Sikes, hearing the noise and shouting, had come out of the public house to see Oliver struggling with Nancy. Bill hit Oliver again, then grabbed him by the collar and began dragging the dazed boy through a maze of

narrow, winding streets to the place Oliver
dreaded even more than he dreaded the
workhouse: Fagin's den.

'Delighted to see you looking so well, my
boy!' Fagin said in that menacing voice
which made Oliver shiver. Oliver shivered
again. He was trapped! His heart sank when
he thought of all his good friends at
Mr Brownlow's house. What would they
think of him when he did not return?
Perhaps they would believe he had run
away with Mr Brownlow's five pounds and
the valuable books, to say nothing of his
fine new suit of clothes.

'If they think that, I could not bear it!'
Oliver reflected, feeling dreadfully upset.

In the next few days, Oliver watched for ways to escape, but Fagin saw to it that he was never alone and had no chance to get away. That meant, of course, that Mr Brownlow, who was frantically searching for Oliver, had no chance of finding him. Mr Brownlow sent out servants to scour the streets for the boy, and asked everyone he could find if they had seen him. The old gentleman even put an advertisement in the newspaper, offering a reward for information about Oliver. But all his efforts achieved nothing. No one knew where Oliver was. As far as Mr Brownlow was concerned, the boy had vanished.

In the meantime, Fagin was trying to train Oliver to be a criminal. He did this by telling Oliver how exciting it was to go out thieving and what a fortune he could make if only he would work hard at it. The Artful Dodger, said Fagin, was a great man because he was such a clever thief.

Oliver did not believe a word of it, but he never let Fagin know that.

At last, Fagin decided he could now trust the boy to help in his criminal work. 'I'm sending you over to Bill Sikes, my boy!' Fagin told Oliver one day. 'We've a nice little job for you, hee, hee, hee!' Fagin cackled, in a sinister way that frightened Oliver.

Nancy came to collect Oliver and take him to Bill Sikes. Oliver noticed that she seemed very upset. Nancy had good reason to feel that way. Despite her rough ways and sharp tongue, she had a kind heart.

She had become very fond of Oliver and hated to see him hurt or in danger. And Oliver was in great danger now, because Fagin and Bill Sikes planned to use him to help them in a big robbery.

Oliver learned of this robbery when he reached Bill's house.

'Do you know what this is?' Bill asked him, pointing to a small pistol which lay on the table in front of him.

Oliver gulped and nodded. Bill picked up the pistol, loaded it with bullets and then placed the barrel against Oliver's head. It felt cold and hard.

'We're going out, you and me,' Sikes growled. 'And if you speak a word to anyone, I'll blow your head off!'

It was not a threat Oliver could easily forget. Bill Sikes was a very violent man, and he meant what he said.

Oliver's journey with Bill Sikes was a long one. It took them some distance from

London to a dank, dilapidated house near a river bank. There, Sikes' two accomplices were waiting for him. After gathering up their pistols, crowbars and other equipment, they all set off into the pitch-black, foggy night.

Oliver now realised the frightful crime in which he was involved, and begged Bill Sikes to let him go.

'I'll never come near London again, never. You'll hear no more of me, I promise!' Oliver cried. 'Please, Mr Sikes, please...'

It was no use. Bill had a job for Oliver to do, and he meant to make sure he did it. They reached the house where the robbery was going to take place, and Bill used his crowbar to force open a small window.

'You're going in there!' he told Oliver. He

pointed to the window, which was so tiny only a boy of Oliver's size could get through it. 'Once you're in,' Bill went on, 'go to the front door and open it to let us in! I'll have this pistol pointing at you all the way, so don't try any tricks — or I'll shoot you dead!'

Despite this threat, Oliver had made up his mind to try to warn the people in the house. Once through the window, he made as if to dart upstairs to the family's rooms, but Bill saw him. He yelled, 'Come back! Back, back, you little wretch!'

Suddenly, there was another cry — from upstairs this time. Two men appeared at the top of the stairs. One of them held a lantern, the other a pistol. Oliver heard him fire it, and felt a fierce hot pain in his arm. Evil-smelling smoke surrounded him. There was a crash, another shot and the sound of a bell clanging loudly. Then Oliver felt himself being lifted up and dragged outside.

The robbery had gone wrong. The two men in the house had raised the alarm, and there was nothing Bill Sikes and his gang could do but run, taking Oliver with them.

As they ran, they heard the shouts of men pursuing them, accompanied by the barking of dogs. Oliver was hardly aware of what was happening. He was dazed and his arm hurt him dreadfully. Then blackness closed in on him and he fainted.

When Oliver awoke, he was lying in a ditch, where Bill Sikes had left him. Bill and the other robbers were nowhere to be seen, for they had all managed to escape the pursuit and hurried back as fast as they could to London. Oliver felt weak and the shawl Bill had tied round his arm was soaked in blood.

With a tremendous effort, Oliver struggled
to his feet and staggered along until he
reached a road. A short way on, he came to
a house. He realised, with a flicker of fear,
that it was the very house where the
robbery had been attempted the previous

night. Oliver wanted to run away, but he could only totter through the gateway and along the path towards the front door.

Inside, in the kitchen, the servants heard a noise. When they opened the front door, one of them, Mr Giles, recognised Oliver at once as the robber he had shot the previous night.

'Here's a thief! I shot him!' Giles shouted triumphantly.

'Giles!' A soft voice whispered from the top of the stairs. 'Hush, or you will frighten my aunt!'

It was a young girl, very slender and sweet-faced, with warm deep blue eyes. She came quietly down the stairs and looked at Oliver, who had been carried inside and was lying on the hall floor.

'Oh, the poor little fellow!' the girl exclaimed. 'Carry him upstairs, Giles! Gently now, be careful!'

Giles obeyed. The young lady, whose name was Rose, ordered the doctor to be brought. The bullet, the doctor discovered, had broken Oliver's arm. It was not a serious injury, but a long time passed before the arm mended and Oliver felt well again.

Rose, her aunt Mrs Maylie, the doctor, whose name was Losberne, and everyone in the house — even Giles — were very kind and gentle towards Oliver. It was almost like being in Mr Brownlow's place again. Oliver was very grateful for his good fortune, but all the same, he wanted more than anything to return to London and find Mr Brownlow.

Dr Losberne offered to take Oliver to London in his carriage. When they reached the street where Mr Brownlow lived, he asked the boy: 'Which house is it? Point it out!'

Oliver spotted the house at once. 'That one! There! The white house!' he cried excitedly.

But Oliver's excitement soon faded. When he looked through the windows, he saw the house was all shut up and the rooms were empty. There was a notice outside saying: 'House to Let.' Dr Losberne sent his coachman next door to enquire after Mr Brownlow, but he returned with sad news. Mr Brownlow, it seemed, had gone away six weeks previously — to the West Indies, far off across the Atlantic Ocean.

Oliver burst into tears. It was all too terrible! Mr Brownlow must have left thinking Oliver was a deceitful, dishonest little wretch. Now he would probably never learn the truth.

For a long time after Dr Losberne had taken Oliver back to his friends in the country, the boy was very sad and depressed. Oliver could not imagine then that there would be a happy ending to his search, but there was. One day, three months later, Dr Losberne took Oliver to London again, and Rose Maylie came with them. They were all delighted to find that Mr Brownlow had now returned to London and was very anxious for news of Oliver. The old gentleman greeted Oliver very warmly.

Mrs Bedwin, the housekeeper, hugged him and kissed him and hugged him again.

'I knew he would come back, I knew it!' she exclaimed joyfully.

When all the greetings were over, and Oliver was well occupied telling Mrs Bedwin of his adventures, Rose made a strange request of Mr Brownlow. She wanted to see him alone, for she had a secret to confide in him. It sounded very important, so Mr Brownlow took Rose to a quiet room, where she told him a very curious tale.

A day or two before, a wretched young girl called Nancy had come to see Rose at her hotel in London. Nancy told Rose about a man called Monks, who had come to Fagin's house a few days previously, while Nancy was there.

Fagin and Monks knew each other very well, for they had planned the robbery at the house where Rose lived with Mrs Maylie. Fagin took the visitor off to another room and Nancy, listening at the door, overheard Monks talking of Oliver. Oliver, Monks said, was his young brother, and he wanted Fagin to arrange to have him killed so that he could get his hands on the boy's fortune.

'I heard Monks mention your name, Miss,' Nancy had explained to Rose. 'And where you were staying in London! That's how I knew where to find you.' Then Nancy started to cry bitterly. 'Please, please, Miss, don't let darling Oliver come to any harm! I'd give my own life if I could to save him, that I would!'

'But what can I do?' Rose had protested. 'How can I find this dreadful Mr Monks?'

'I can help you!' Nancy said. 'If you'll find a gentleman to help and protect you, I'll tell

you where Monks can be found.'

'But where shall we meet you?' Rose
wanted to know.

'On London Bridge. I'll be there every
Sunday night, between eleven and
midnight,' Nancy had promised.

Mr Brownlow was astonished and intrigued by Rose's story.

'There's a mystery here, right enough!' he murmured. 'And we'll never get to the bottom of it unless we can get hold of this scoundrel Monks. Nancy will lead us to him, you say?'

'Yes,' Rose told him.

Mr Brownlow tapped his chin, thinking hard. 'This girl Nancy is taking a great risk for Oliver's sake. She's a very brave soul,' he muttered at length.

'The thieves and criminals who are her companions will surely kill her if they discover what she has done.'

Mr Brownlow sighed. 'But we cannot let this chance slip by. After all, Oliver's fortune and his life, too, are at stake. No, we must meet this girl and learn all we can from her!'

Nancy was unable to go to London Bridge on the first Sunday night, for Bill Sikes, who was in a very bad mood, threatened to beat her if she left the house.

Fagin was there at the time and he thought there was something very odd about Nancy's manner and behaviour. Why did she want to go out?

Fagin was curious. He decided to send one of his boys to follow Nancy on the next Sunday night, to see where she went and who she met.

The boy spy faithfully carried out Fagin's instructions. He saw Nancy meet Rose and Mr Brownlow on the bridge just after midnight. Unseen and unheard, the spy crept close and heard Nancy describe the tall, lean Mr Monks, the public house he often visited and the times he went there.

'You can recognise him easily,' Nancy said. 'There is a mark on his throat, a big, red...'

'A red mark!' Mr Brownlow interrupted her. 'A mark like a burn or a scald?'

Rose and Nancy exchanged surprised looks.

'Why, yes!' Nancy replied. 'Do you know him, sir?'

Mr Brownlow nodded. There was a grim expression on his face. 'Yes, yes, I think I do!' he muttered.

*　　*　　*

Mr Brownlow lost no time. The very next day, he went out with two of his menservants to look for Monks. Quite near the public house Nancy had spoken of, they spotted their prey. Before Monks knew what was happening, he was grabbed by the menservants, bundled into a hackney carriage and driven off at a smart pace to Mr Brownlow's house.

There, Monks was led to a back room.

'Go outside and lock the door!'
Mr Brownlow told the menservants.
'Mr Monks and I will speak together alone!'

The two men looked doubtful, for Monks
seemed dangerous. Nevertheless, they
obeyed.

When they had gone, Mr Brownlow
looked at Monks sadly for a few moments.

'I thought this was the man. He's the son
of my best friend,' Mr Brownlow reflected.
'Poor Nancy described him well...' Then
Mr Brownlow said aloud: 'Your name is not
Monks, is it? It's Edward Leeford!'

Monks gave a start of surprise. 'How
d'you know that?' he growled suspiciously.

Mr Brownlow sighed. 'Because I knew
your father Edwin Leeford, and his sister,
who died many, many years ago on the very
day she and I were to be married!'

A flicker of pain crossed Mr Brownlow's
face as he remembered his young, dead
bride-to-be. He had not spoken of her to
anyone for a very long time. 'I know that
your father and mother were unhappy
together,' he went on, 'and that they parted
when you were still a young boy! And,'

Mr Brownlow paused for a second, 'I know you have a brother!'

Monks' eyes narrowed. 'I have no brother! I was an only child!'

'The only child of your father's marriage, yes!' said Mr Brownlow. 'But after your parents parted, your father fell in love with a beautiful young girl called Agnes Fleming. Poor Agnes died giving birth to their child. It was a boy who, by the grace of God, later fell into my hands! I knew what Agnes looked like, you see, for your father gave me her portrait and the boy looked exactly like her!'

By this time, Monks was utterly
dumbfounded by Mr Brownlow's revelations.
However, the old gentleman had not yet
finished. He told how Oliver Twist had
disappeared on the way to the bookshop,
and how he had searched high and low for
him without success.

'I knew you could solve this mystery for
me,' Mr Brownlow told Monks. 'I also knew
of your criminal life and that you had
escaped to the West Indies. So I followed
you there!'

The long voyage to the Indies had been
fruitless. By the time Mr Brownlow had

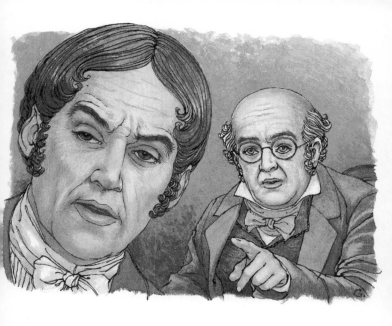

arrived there, Monks had already returned to
England. Mr Brownlow made the long
journey home again, and scoured the streets
seeking Monks for many weeks. But not
until he heard Nancy speak of him did the
old gentleman have any clue to where
Monks could be found.

'You were a wretched child, and you are
still the scoundrel and robber you always
were!' Mr Brownlow accused Monks. 'You
plan to have young Oliver murdered, don't
you, so that you can have all your father's
money!'

'You can't prove anything against me!' Monks blustered, turning very pale.

'Oh, but I can!' Mr Brownlow retorted. 'I know about Fagin and the plot you have hatched together...'

'F-Fagin?' Monks stuttered. 'I know no such man...'

'Shall we call the police, then, and let you deny it to them?'

Monks looked terrified at that. 'No, no, don't... I must not fall into the hands of the police... they will... hang me!'

Mr Brownlow gave a sigh of satisfaction. 'Ah, then, you will surely do as I demand!' he cried. 'You must sign a document giving Oliver his rightful inheritance − his share of your father's money!'

Monks looked thoroughly miserable. He thought of the police cell, the courtroom and the hangman's rope that would undoubtedly be round his neck if he refused.

'Very well,' he muttered resentfully. 'Oliver shall have his inheritance − I promise!'

Poor Nancy, whose love for Oliver made her take such great risks on his behalf, would have been very happy to know of the boy's good fortune. But sadly, Nancy had

paid a high price for her actions. When the
young spy told Fagin about Nancy's meeting
with Rose and Mr Brownlow on London
Bridge, Fagin had been enraged. He sent for
Bill Sikes and told him the story. Bill, always
a brutal man, took his pistol and shot Nancy
dead.

Even as Mr Brownlow and Monks were talking, the police were out hunting for the murderer. That very night, they cornered Bill Sikes in his hiding place. In a panic, Bill clambered out onto the roof, taking with him a rope to let himself down to the ground and so get away. But he missed his footing and as he fell, the rope tangled round his neck. The rope tightened, and Bill choked to death.

That same day, acting on information given to them by Mr Brownlow, the police arrested Fagin, together with several of his boy thieves. At his trial, Fagin was condemned to death for all his crimes. He later ended his disreputable life on the hangman's gallows.

As for Oliver Twist, Mr Brownlow adopted him as his son. He took him to live in the country, with the housekeeper Mrs Bedwin. Oliver was very happy there, for he loved the fresh green countryside, with its beautiful fields and flowers and trees.

Once, Oliver had been a poor misused orphan boy whose only home was the workhouse. Now, his future was bright and life offered him much happiness. He had the inheritance his father had intended for him. Above all, now that Fagin was dead and his gang of thieves and killers broken up, Oliver need never be afraid of them again.